I Love You So...

by
Marianne Richmond

sourcebooks
jabberwocky

I Love You So...

LCCN 2004115278

Published by Sourcebooks Jabberwocky,
an imprint of Sourcebooks, Inc.
P.O. Box 4410
Naperville, IL 60567-4410
(630) 961-3900
www.sourcebooks.com

Illustrations by Marianne Richmond

Book design by Sara Dare Biscan

Source of Production: Toppan Leefung
Printers (Dongguan) Limited,
Dongguan City, Guangdong Province, China
Date of Production: April 2014
Run Number: 5001261

Printed in China
TPL 10 9

Available everywhere books are sold
from author & illustrator
Marianne Richmond:

If I Could Keep You Little

I'm Not Tired Yet

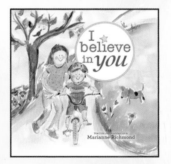

I Believe in You

**Oh, the Things My
Mom Will Do....**

I Love You So...

is dedicated to

Cole James, Adam Jon, Julia Rose, and Will David,
who fill my heart with gigantic love. — MR

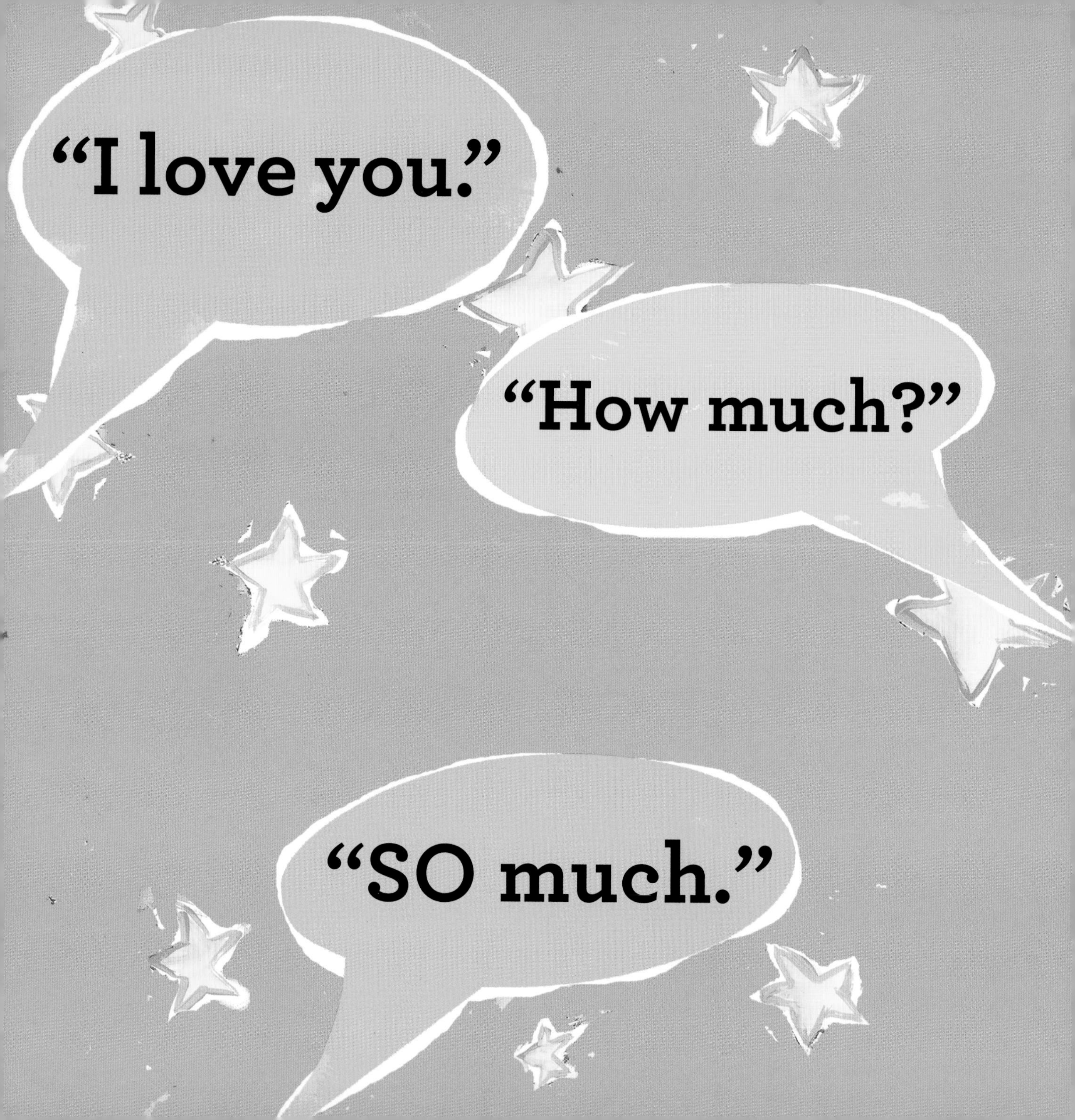
"I love you."
"How much?"
"SO much."

"How much is 'so'?"

"Way, way more than you know..."

I love you as **BRILLIANT**
as each sparkling star,
and as **WAY OUT** as space,
I love you **THAT** far.

Marshmallows

I love you as GIGANTIC
as a great lion's roar,
and as DEEP as the ocean,
I love you MUCH more.

"That IS a lot," you say,
"but HOW did it start?
WHERE did love come from
to be in your heart?"

YOU put it there, really,
when you and I met.
And I knew for certain
WITHOUT you I'd fret.

From MY HEAD to my TOES,
I was feeling inside
a devotion for you
SO DEEP and SO WIDE.

And now it's ENORMOUS
and wonderfully real
and hard to describe
HOW MUCH I feel!

Girl power

15

I love you as AWESOME
as a thundery sky,
and as SOARING as mountains,
I love you THAT high.

"Do you love me EVERY day?"
you ask with doubting awe,
"or does love go UP 'N DOWN
like a teetering see-saw?"

I love you as **STEADY**
as the earth rounds the sun,
though **SOME** days of life
are the **FARTHEST** from fun.

"Like when you feel MAD?"
    you ask with distress,
"'cause I've BROKEN the rules
    or made a BIG mess?

"Or, when I'm UNKIND,
    and your feelings are BLUE,
do you love me ALTHOUGH
    I do what I do?"

I love you being NICE,
    and when you're CRANKY, too.
I love you without liking
    the NAUGHTY things you do.

My 'love you' DOESN'T change like the temper of the days. It's a CERTAIN kind of thing in many DIFFERENT ways.

Hanging out WITH YOU
is where I want to be...
eating ice cream sundaes
or watching the TV.

UNDER your umbrella,
behind you on a bike.
BY you and BESIDE you
is what I REALLY like.

"Do you love me just AS MUCH when I'm FAR away from home? Is your loving still THE SAME in distant lands I roam?"

I love you NEAR or FAR.
I love you HIGH or LOW.
My love is there with you
WHEREVER you may go.

"Even when I'm SICK...
    and I can't get out of bed?
Do you love me better HEALTHY
    than with fever in my head?"

I love you sick or able.
You're ALWAYS you to me,
the ONE I LOVE forevermore.
Undeniably.

I CAN'T IMAGINE life
before YOU came along...
me there singing senseless,
no MEANING to my song.

Call it MEANT TO BE
or simply blessed fate,
you fill my heart WITH LOVE...
and for THAT I celebrate.

"I love you."

"How much?"

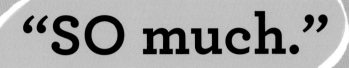

"**WAY**, WAY MORE than you know..."

Marianne Richmond has touched the lives of millions
for nearly two decades through her award-winning books,
greeting cards, and other gift products that offer people the
most heartfelt way to connect.